Pound Puppies

Lovable, Huggable
Public Nuisance

By Justine Korman
Illustrated by Pat Paris

A GOLDEN BOOK • NEW YORK
Western Publishing Company, Inc., Racine, Wisconsin 53404

"Come out with your hands up. This is the law!" shouted Gumshoe Gallagher on the TV screen in the Pound Puppies' mission control room.

"You tell him, Gumshoe!" exclaimed Cooler, cheering on his hero, Police Detective Gallagher.

Cooler looked up when Bright Eyes burst into the room. She had a nose for news around the Pound, and it looked like she had a scoop.

"Cooler, there's a new puppy who has come to stay at the Pound," Bright Eyes exclaimed.

Cooler switched off the TV. Gumshoe Gallagher or no, as leader of the Pound Puppies, it was his duty to welcome new arrivals.

"Oh, and by the way, it's Dogcatcher Nabbit's birthday," Bright Eyes added. "And he's ever so sad because no one remembered."

Cooler peeked into the Pound office and saw the new puppy being registered. The puppy looked nice but was wearing a muzzle over its mouth. There was a police officer with the puppy. The officer declared, "He's a public nuisance! He barked and barked all day until everyone in the neighborhood called to complain."

When the new puppy, Bogart, came into the Pound yard, Cooler introduced him to the rest of the gang. "Are you a stray?" Bright Eyes asked gently.

"I'm a public nuisance," Bogart replied angrily. "At least that's what they think. But I had a reason for barking so much."

"You can tell us," Cooler urged. "Maybe we can help."

"I'm a stray," Bogart began. "I've been one all my life. I was snooping around a quiet neighborhood, looking for scraps, when I heard someone crying.

"I followed the sound to a gardening shed behind one of the houses. When I looked through a knothole in the wood, I saw a beautiful cat," the puppy said. "She told me her name was Simone and that she was a rare prize-winning show cat. She said she had been cat-napped and was being held for ransom.

"Simone wasn't that worried about herself. She was more worried about her owners, a rich old lady and her grandson, Sam," Bogart said. "It made me wonder what it would be like to have a real home with people who love you."

Violet sniffled, and Scrounger added a sad "A-woo!"

"I tried to get the shed door open, but it wouldn't budge," Bogart continued.

"So I started barking, hoping someone would come to see what all the noise was about," Bogart explained. "The cat-nappers chased me away a couple of times, but I kept going back.

"All the neighbors got angry," Bogart said. "But no one came to see what was the matter. They called the police, who brought me here. Now they're calling me a public nuisance, and Simone is still trapped in that shed."

"That's the saddest story I ever heard," Bright Eyes said as she wiped her eyes with the back of her paws.

"We'll help that cat!" Cooler said. Then he rubbed his chin thoughtfully. "And I think I've got just the plan," he added.

Bogart and the other Pound Puppies gathered in a huddle to hear Cooler's plan.

"Violet, Scrounger, Bogart, and I will work on Mission Rescue," Cooler concluded. "Bright Eyes, Howler, and the rest of you will be in charge of Operation Decoy."

Scrounger quickly gathered the necessary materials: flashlights, cardboard, paint, a tape recorder, a loudspeaker, party hats, crepe paper, a birthday cake, and candles.

Meanwhile, Bright Eyes and Howler held a loud conversation near the nasty guard dogs.

"I just can't wait for our big escape tonight," Bright Eyes declared.

"Shh! Itchey and Snitchey might be eavesdripping... eavesdrumming...I mean listening," Howler howled.

That night the Mission Rescue team crept out of the
Pound through secret Pound Puppies tunnels. Finally they
reached the house where Bogart had seen the cat-
nappers. They surrounded the house, and when Cooler
gave the signal, the Pound Puppies turned on their
flashlights, the tape recorder, and the loudspeaker.

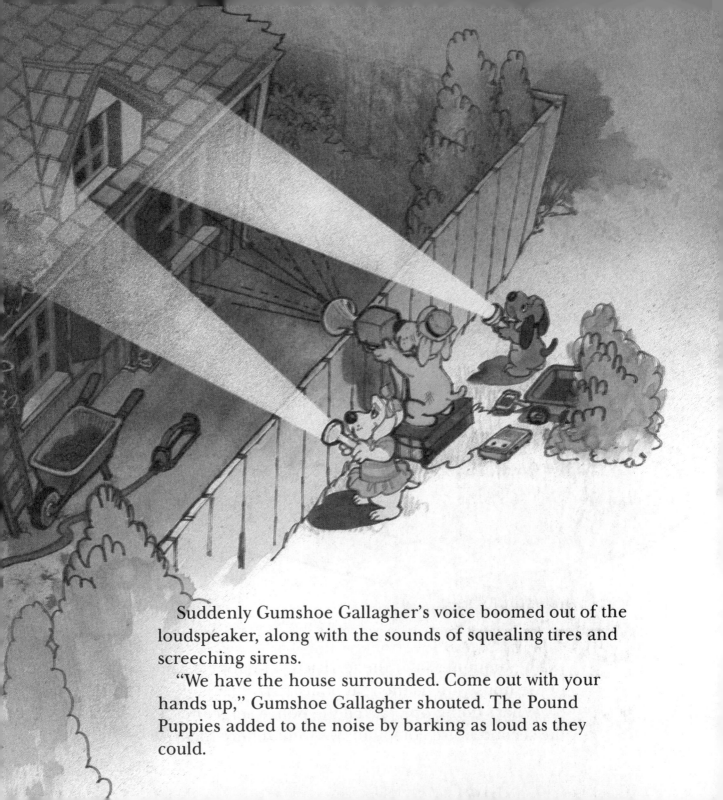

Suddenly Gumshoe Gallagher's voice boomed out of the loudspeaker, along with the sounds of squealing tires and screeching sirens.

"We have the house surrounded. Come out with your hands up," Gumshoe Gallagher shouted. The Pound Puppies added to the noise by barking as loud as they could.

A few minutes later the terrified cat-nappers came out of the house just as the real police arrived.

"What's going on?" asked the police sergeant. "This is the second noise complaint we've had here today."

The Pound Puppies led the police officers to the shed where Simone was held captive.

"It's that missing show cat!" the sergeant exclaimed.

Within minutes Simone's worried owners were brought to the scene, and the cat-nappers were under arrest.

Bogart was no longer a public nuisance—he was a hero!

Simone purred happily as Sam, the little boy, stroked her fur. Then Sam walked over to Bogart and gave him a big hug. Bogart wagged his tail excitedly. It was puppy love at first sight.

"You can come home with us," Sam's grandmother told Bogart. Then she invited the Pound Puppies to come to her house to celebrate Simone's return.

But the Pound Puppies had a date to keep at the Pound.

Meanwhile, back at the Pound, Itchey and Snitchey
wanted to tell Nabbit about the big escape. They led him
to the Pound Puppies' room, but they were met with
happy birthday barks.

Bright Eyes, Howler, and the other Pound Puppies had
arranged a big surprise party in honor of Nabbit's
birthday. Itchey and Snitchey were quite confused.

Everyone was having such a good time, it took a while for Nabbit to notice that some of the puppies were missing.

"Where's Cooler?" Nabbit asked, looking around. "And Violet and…"

Before Nabbit could ask any more questions, Bright Eyes put a blindfold over his eyes to play pin the tail on the puppy. Then Howler distracted Itchey and Snitchey with huge pieces of birthday cake.

That gave Cooler, Scrounger, and Violet enough time to sneak back into the Pound—right into the middle of the party.

"Where did you…" Nabbit muttered as he pulled the blindfold from his eyes.

Cooler winked, then congratulated the rest of the gang. "Another case solved—thanks to the Pound Puppies."